TICKLE HEART
VOLUME 2

A COLLECTION OF FUNNY SHORT STORIES

Paolo Debernardi

ISBN 978-1-0683558-0-6 (Pbk)
ISBN 978-1-0683558-1-3 (e-book)

Printed by Biddles Books Limited,
King's Lynn, Norfolk

Contents

Introduction

Since the publication of "**Tickle Heart Vol.1**", I have written a second volume full of funny English stories so, when you are feeling sad or you have received some bad news, pick one story and it will bright up your day. I want to make people smile. Laughter is the best medicine.

Compared to the first volume, I have done more research; what is trendy and funny in social media, and I had more funny ideas. Writing funny short stories is much harder than other stories; they must be shorter, otherwise, if the story has too many pages when I tell the punch line it is not funny anymore.

I am also extending volume one, because more funny stories came in my mind.

I want to thank Hannah Curtis and Andrew Thornton for creating the book cover.

In this book, you will find part of the writing as ***Bold Italic***, this part represents the character's thoughts and Comic Sans is the animal talking.

Special guests are: Spiderman, Captain America, Darth Vader, Luke Skywalker, Human Torch, The invisible woman, Aquaman and Chewbacca.

After reading this book, please visit Amazon.co.uk or Amazon.com and write a review.

Please go to the following link for competitions, book releases, and latest updates of Paolo Debernardi's TV, film, and theatre appearances:

https://form.aweber.com/form/11/351188711.htm

The Author
Paolo Debernardi

Me vs the hare

On a Sunday afternoon, I was driving in my BMW Series 3 on a new stretch of motorway, which was built to facilitate easier driving and to ease congestions and car accidents instead of using the dual carriageway. I was taking my friend Frank to his house. I checked the speedometer; the car was going 70 miles per hour.

Something overtook us. There was no sound and it was not a vehicle.

"What was that?"

"I have no idea, Frank."

I accelerated to 90 miles per hour. My car was now alongside the object which had passed us.

"You won't believe it; it is a hare."

"It is a supersonic hare."

"I agree, Frank."

I overtook it.

The hare was not pleased, and it repassed my car. For 3 miles we and the hare were changing positions between first and second. I looked outside and noticed the final exit was in half mile away.

Without a minute to spare, I flattened the pedal brake, and the car halted.

"What happened to the hare, John?"

"I am not sure, Frank."

I was driving very slowly, and I saw a pair of ears on the asphalt.

I picked them up after opening my car door.

"Where is the rest of the body?"

"Imagine a hare needed to slow down at high speed by using only his bottom to decelerate. My guess is his body has burnt up."

John vs the Alien

John entered the bedroom.

"Who are you?"

"Don't be shy, I am not going to hurt you. I am civilised."

"Ok, I'm breaking the ice. My name is John, and I am coming from Proxima B, 4.22 light years away." He pointed at the stranger.

"Awesome, you are coming from Proxima B too. I thought I was the only alien on this planet Earth. We can have many conversations about Proxima B. In which city did you use to live?"

"You are not very talkative. I am not going to bite you."

"Who are you talking to, John?" "Are you losing the plot?"

"No Louise, I am perfectly fine. I have been talking to another alien in our bedroom."

"John, there is only me and you in this apartment. I don't know any other alien apart from you."

"Come into the bedroom, I will show you."

Louise entered the bedroom.

"So, you can see, there is another alien in front of me."

"You are silly, John. That is your reflection in the mirrored wardrobe."

"Really, I am looking awesome." While he was blowing kisses to his own reflection.

"Great, my boyfriend is a narcissist!"

The unexpected visit

Ding-dong ding-dong

"Wait a minute, I'm coming. People are no longer patient these days."

Jessica walked to the front door and opened it wide.

"OMG! You frightened me, nice costume by the way."

The Grim Reaper was standing close to the front door wielding a scythe.

"How can I help you?"

"I am looking for George Brown."

"I knew him, he used to live here. He was a lovely man. You just missed him."

"Where is he?"

"He is in the same place for the last 2 years. He is in the cemetery."

"Cemetery?"

"Yes, it is a place where all the dead people are. His family bought a pine coffin for his body to be buried by the gravedigger."

"Nobody told me anything."

"I feel your pain. I can't stand being the last person finding out everything that's going on."

"Do you know Matthew White?"

"Yes, I do. He is a very kind man who spends his spare time in charity shops. He lives at 23 Queen Street. My house is number 17. It's just 3 doors down that way." pointing to the left.

The Grim Reaper pointed to the left with his skeleton slim index finger.

"That's right!"

Jessica slammed the front door.

"Darling, who was it?"

"He was a weirdo asking about George Brown and Matthew White wearing a Halloween costume on 15 October. Every year, people are getting weirder and frightening me to death. That was the scariest Grim Reaper I have seen in my life."

The peculiar poker game

Every Friday evening, John Brown enjoys playing Texas hold 'em with his friends. This poker game is very peculiar. John is playing against Chris who is his deaf best friend, and Stuart is blind.

During a hand, Chris is small blind, and Stuart is big blind, and John is the dealer. The blinds are £20 and £40. Because Stuart cannot see the cards, John had created playing cards with braille to identify which card and suit are.

"I call" John is the first to act.

Chris replaces £20 with £40; it is his way to say call.

Stuart taps the table indicating check.

The flop comes down as Ace, Queen, Jack of clubs, all three players tap the table.

The turn is Ace of spade, all three players tap the table.

The river is Seven of diamonds. Chris and Stuart tap the table.

"I'm all in!" John exclaims.

"I call you!" Chris exclaims.

"I see you both!" Stuart adds.

John has four Aces; Chris has a full house, Queens over Aces and Stuart has a Royal Flush of clubs.

"For a blind person, I don't know how you do it. You are the luckiest person I have ever played against."

Trilemma

"Hit me"

"Sir, what is your poison?"

"Three shots of Scotch whisky with two ice cubes in a whisky glass, please"

"Tough day?"

"You can say that."

The bartender poured three shots of whisky and two ice cubes in the glass and placed it in front of the punter.

"Thank you. I needed this."

"I am a good listener. I might be able to help you if you can confide with me."

"Ok, my name is John Walker. I am in a difficult situation. I have trilemma."

"I beg you, pardon. What is a trilemma?"

"I have coined a new word. Trilemma is a situation in which a difficult choice has to be made between three alternatives that are equally undesirable."

"Have you ever served a man called George Brown?"

"Yes, I have. He used to be a regular punter in this establishment. I have not seen him for the last 4 months."

"I met him too, 6 months ago. He was seated on a bench in the back of the pub. His head was supported by his hands in a gloomy expression. I approached him."

"Is this seat taken?"

"No. I am not a good company tonight. I am facing difficult times."

"I understand. My name is John Walker."

"Nice to meet you. I'm George Brown."

"So, what is the matter?"

"I'm working very hard every day and with the recession and cost of living, it seems there is just enough money to pay my rent and utility bills and at the end of the month I have nothing left in my bank account. I wish someone could believe in me. I have an idea which could change my financial situation; however, no banks or financial institutions would lend me any money due to my low income and my outgoings."

"You are in luck. My job is lending money to individuals or businesses which other banks or financial institutions reject. If you could pitch me your idea, I will see what I can do for you."

George Brown pitched his brilliant idea demonstrating he had already a list of buyers wanting to order his new product.

"I think your idea has legs and you only need £2000 to get started. It is durable and you can pay back within 3 years with interest. I can offer you the lowest interest rate to help you out."

"You are my saviour. You don't know how much it means to me. I promise I will pay back the capital and interest and in case the business fails, I will sell my three-year-old black Mustang as collateral."

"I believe in you George. We will meet up every Friday in this establishment at 5 p.m. and you can start repaying the loan in a fortnight."

"I agree, thank you so much John Walker."

For the first three weeks, George Brown was paying the capital plus interest without an issue. The following Friday, John visited the pub and stayed until closing time. George Brown did not turn up. The following day John called and emailed George. He didn't answer. Every Friday, John visited the establishment, there was no sign of George. John was becoming suspicious George was ghosting him. In the loan application, George had provided his home address, and he was aware George was married to Sheila, who was a nymphomaniac. After the latest missed appointment by George, John took courage and turned up in front of his house.

Knock knock

"Just a minute, I'm coming." Sheila opened the front door wearing a mini skirt and a tight top holding her breast from popping out.

"I'm John Walker and I'm looking for George."

"George told me lots of about you. He is currently out. He just texted me and he will be back in 2 hours. If you want to wait, you can come in."

"Are you sure I am not imposing?"

"Of course not, what is your poison?"

"Could I have a shot of scotch whisky with some ice cubes?"

"I fetch your drink, please take a seat in this armchair."

"Thank you."

"You look so tense."

"I am. I have been worried sick. George has missed so many appointments and he is in arrears with the loan."

"He told me, the business took off better than he expected. He quit his job. He is fully concentrated on the business, and he is making so much money. Let me give you a body massage. I'm a professional masseuse."

Sheila started to massage his shoulders.

"You are very tense. Let's loosen up these muscles."

"That is nice."

Sheila kissed John's cheek. John kissed her cheek. They snogged. The sexual chemistry sparked between them. Sheila took off all his clothes and John took off the few clothes she was wearing. She took his hand, and they walked into the bedroom. She was lying down, and he was on top. They were having sex when two manly hands began touching John's chest, and something was touching his bottom. The stranger was in fact George, who was giving him sex from behind. At the end of the evening, John was confused and disturbed. The following Friday, John was waiting again in the establishment for George, but he did not arrive. He decided to visit again George's house. This time, when Sheila opened the door, she was wearing a dressing gown. She gave him a massage and they ended up sleeping together in the bedroom. Again, George turned up and made love to John as before.

Every Friday, it was becoming a routine. John was more confused and disturbed.

"I'm in a trilemma. Every Friday I come here expecting George will pay me, he never turns up then I go to his house where his wife makes love to me, and later George arrives and has sex with me from behind."

"I see, no matter how you look at it, you have been screwed front, back and sideways."

"I don't think I will see my money back."

John picked up the glass and swallowed the whisky hoping it would allow him to forget the horrible experience.

BMW vs Ferrari

In a traffic light intersection, the red light was illuminated. A BMW 3 series was side by side with a Ferrari 308 GTO.

Brrrrum **Brrrrum** **Brrrrum**, the BMW 3 series was revving the roaring engine.

Vroom vroom vroom, the Ferrari 308 GTO replied with its revving subdued engine.

The amber traffic light illuminated together with the red light.

Brrrrum **Brrrrum** **Brrrrum**, the BMW 3 series was revving the roaring engine.

Vroom vroom vroom, the Ferrari 308 GTO replied with its revving subdued engine.

They were replaced by the green light in a matter of seconds. The Ferrari 308 GTO had already driven down the main road while the BMW 3 series had stalled the engine. The other drivers were fuming and cursing at the incompetent driver.

Beep beep beep

"Let's go"

"You are all noise, but no speed."

"Even my 90-year-old grandmother is faster than you!"

Not a happy bunny

It was the Easter weekend; the DJ was playing the current trendy songs. There were many people showing the best moves on the dance floor. Everyone made an effort to dress for the occasion. A young woman was wearing a white rabbit costume with bunny ears. She approached the DJ hopping. She begged him to play her favourite song, but he refused firmly.

She stared down with a gloomy expression walking away.

Paul Robinson approached the DJ greeting him with a fist bump.

"What is wrong with her?"

"She asked me to play "Can You Feel It" by the Jacksons. I said no. I have already played this song 3 times in the last hour."

"Fair enough, she is not a happy bunny."

Weird conversations in a poker game

Every season of every year John knocked Peter out of the poker tournaments. **"Tonight, I am going to show John, I am his bitch!"**

"John, tonight I am taking you out."

"Awesome, Peter, where are we going? I like fine restaurants, or I would love to go to Silverstone. I am a big fan of Formula One. I have been watching since I was 10 years old."

"No John, you misunderstood me. Let's me rephrase that. You are going down."

"I have never gone down on my first date, and I will never have sex with a man. I am only interested in women."

"Okay, I am going to be crystal clear. Tonight, I will steal all your poker chips!"

"Stealing is a criminal offence, and you will be arrested. Just to let you know, I have taken out insurance against theft."

"Never mind, John, Jack has just knocked me out of the tournament."

"Bummer, I was looking forward to dating. It has been more than sixteen years since last time. Jack always spoils everything"

Car enthusiasts

After a day of work, four best friends meet up in Yates. It is their favourite local pub and a daily traditional routine.

"Today, it is my round. I have discovered there is a correlation between cars and drivers."

"Tell us, PierAngelo."

"I'm driving a 512BB red Ferrari, because Italian people are passionate about these sporty red cars. I like the acceleration and craftmanship of the bodywork."

"Great PierAngelo, I'm driving a black EQE Saloon Mercedes-Benz."

"Brilliant John, it tells me you like luxury items. You always wear Armani suit and a gold Rolex. You want to make a statement."

"That is right!"

"What about me? I'm driving a Lamborghini diablo."

"Well Peter, it tells me you enjoy driving fast and it explains why your hair is always spiky and you have a long red pointed tail."

"You got it."

"What about me? I'm not like you, guys. My car is simple and compact. I am driving a smart EQ forfour."

"That is okay, Andrew, we already know you're a data nerd. Your head is immersed in books every day and when you are not, you google information to acquire knowledge, but, I was not aware your car is intelligent and goes to school."

"Like me, my car always wants to be ahead of everyone."

Smart TV

The sliding doors creaked; John entered Curry's the retail store in York. He was wandering like an idiot in the aisle of TV sets.

A saleswoman approached him.

"Hello sir, how may I be of assistance?"

"Hello Michelle, my family and friends have been nagging me for ages that I should upgrade my TV. I still have a 70's retro television set. It works perfectly, my friends insisted I should check out the smart TV in your store."

"Well sir, this model is the most popular in the consumers' report, and it has all the latest advanced technologies compared with all the TV sets in circulation."

"Let's put it to the test. I'm going to ask you three simple questions. Firstly, can you tell me all the colours of the rainbow?"

Three minutes passed and the smart TV set didn't reply.

"I guess that was difficult for you. Okay, can you tell me the capital of England?"

Three minutes passed and again the smart TV set didn't reply.

"I am a bit disappointed, however my final question is easy. Even my son knows the answer. It is a mathematical question; what is two plus two?"

Three minutes passed and the smart TV didn't answer.

"That is terrible, everyone knows it's four."

John picked up a sticker from his pocket trouser. The image was a boy's head wearing a donkey hat and underneath the boy's head, a caption exclaimed 'you're a dumb!' John applied the sticker to the smart TV set.

"I don't understand all the fuss about smart TV! My retro television set has never let me down!"

John walked out of the store and Michelle never saw him again.

Special army unit

Richard White was part of a special army unit involved in secret missions and saved the country on many occasions. He felt he was making a difference and for thirty years he did not hold back, but his body was craving for a slow pace, so he retired. He enjoyed being active, he jogged for miles in his neighbourhood until he had a stroke. Now he was dragging his feet slowly supported by his walking stick. Every day, a single task was daunting. The best part of the week was Tuesday afternoon. It was his weekly routine to do the shopping. He parked his blue Ford Fiesta in the supermarket's car park, which was on a slope.

An hour later Richard was trudging pushing a shopping trolley to where his car had been parked before; it had just been stolen by four young adults. Richard stepped inside the shopping trolley, which was sliding and zigzagging on the car park, avoiding pedestrians and parked cars; chasing the getaway car. From his observations, he calculated the direction of the vehicle. He made it, he was in front of his blue Ford Fiesta like a Mexican standoff. His Ford Fiesta was boxed in by Richard, the queue of cars behind and the parked cars on its left and right. His car had no way out.

Richard stepped out of the shopping trolley and took out from his backpack an unassembled sniper rifle. In thirty seconds, he assembled it. He smiled, he felt lucky, he was wearing his favourite t-shirt, which had a warning caption: *In my thirty years in the special army unit, I never missed a target.*

"Punks, get out of my car!"

"He is not serious, is he?"

"Guys, it's not worth being shot or killed for stealing a car!"

The four young adults stepped out of the car and fled the scene.

"Mission accomplished!"

Richard approached his car. He pulled out his car key from his trouser pocket. He attempted to start the engine. The car key was too small. He pressed the 'unlock' button.

The click of an unlocked car was heard eleven feet away. It was another parked blue Ford Fiesta surrounded by almost thirty identical cars.

"Tomorrow, I will ask my friend George, who works in a paint shop, to spray my car with a Union Jack!"

Have you been in car accident?

Tring, tring

"Hello."

"Good morning, John Smith. How are you? My name is Claire Simpson."

"How do you know my name?"

"We know everything about you. We are an insurance company. You have a car, and you were in a car accident last month."

"No, I wasn't. I don't have even a car."

"Okay, that is weird. Have you been in a car accident as a passenger within the last six months?"

"No, again, you are wrong. The Greys, who are one of the alien civilizations, brought me back last night after they had abducted me for ten months."

Latest scam phone call

John and Andrew meet up in the street.

"Hi John, how are you?"

"Great, thank you, Andrew."

"Have you heard about the latest scam phone call?"

"Are you talking about the Amazon scam?"

"No, that is an old one. I am talking about the police scam. I received a phone call that the police had an arrest warrant out for me."

"Oh, my goodness, did the police come to your door?"

"No, Andrew, I have been waiting for the last 10 months. I knew it was a scam. The police would never contact a criminal and inform him that, they will arrest him next day at 2 p.m. Even if they did, the criminal would reply: 2 p.m. is not good for me. I have a barber appointment tomorrow, could you change it to 4 p.m.? Of course, I can. The criminal will add: do you think I am stupid? I will be anywhere else but, home."

Misunderstanding in the supermarket

It was a Thursday afternoon, a weekly routine for doing the shopping, James King was in the fruit and veg aisle.

"Those are great round melons. Do they smell okay?"

A woman turned her ahead to her right, she checked if she had farted.

"I beg your pardon. Are you commenting on my bottom? Are you implying I am fat?"

"No, madam. I was talking to that bloke, who is holding two melons!"

"Okay, I forgive you."

Ten minutes later, James was staring at something.

"These are very small juicy and firm."

"How dare you! Apologise at once, what you just said is very insulting. Not every woman has the same size!"

"I didn't mean…"

Smack

The young woman slapped James' face.

"Why did you slap me? I was not talking about your breasts. I was referring to these red Gala apples. They are so juicy and firm."

"I'm sorry, sir. I misunderstood you."

The toilet

It was July and it was getting hotter every day. John and Andrew were male models, living in London. They had been hired for a fashion show in Glasgow on 20 July, which was Saturday. After evaluating all the possible options, they decided to travel by train from King's Cross station to Glasgow Central. The train would take eight hours to reach destination, so they were able to relax and enjoy the journey. John had bought in advance several bottles of water knowing it would be a hot day, and the water would quench them both.

On the day of travel, it was midday, they walked onto the train and sat in the reserved seats.

"John, I need to tell you something, please don't be offended"

"Okay, go ahead, Andrew"

"Someone laughed behind your back about the way you walk on the catwalk."

"What is funny about my walk?"

"Show me and I will tell you, John."

John stood up and walked along the aisle of the carriage.

"Thank you for sharing. Now let me show you, how it should be done."

Andrew walked along the aisle with an attitude.

Lots of women cheered and whistled.

"I will copy your walk."

"Awesome."

During the journey, John couldn't stop drinking the water and he felt it was time to visit the facilities.

John walked along the aisle.

"Is that your new walk, John?"

"No, I need to pee."

John went through to where the toilet was, in the nest carriage. A woman was standing outside waiting for her turn.

"Hello, are you next?"

"Oh, no, I am waiting for my son. He is almost finished."

"It's funny, the toilet is engaged, and I didn't even know it was seeing someone!"

Hide and seek

"Today, we are playing an old children's game. It is called hide and seek. I am going to close my eyes, and I will count up to one hundred while the players are hiding. Then I open my eyes and find the hiders. The players are me, an ordinary man, Spiderman, Captain America, Darth Vader and Luke Skywalker."

John turned his body toward the wall. His head was leaning on his arm. He started to count loudly.

"One two three four … ninety-seven, ninety-eight, ninety-nine, one hundred, ready or not, here I come!"

John turned his body around with his eyes wide open.

"Kooooooo-pah, kooooooo-pah."

"I can hear someone, yes it's Darth Vader hiding behind the sofa."

"No, I'm not."

"Yes, you are, I can hear your heavy breathing. One down, three to seek out."

John noticed something.

"Luke Skywalker, you are behind the frosted glass."

"No, I am not, John. You are cheating, you have X-ray vision"

"No, I haven't. You have forgotten to switch off your lightsabre. It is illuminating the frosted glass. Two people have been found. The next two are difficult to seek."

John paid so much attention and noticed something peculiar on the column.

"I got you, Spiderman. You are behind that column."

"You are wrong, John."

"There are only two possibilities: a spider had been busy spinning webs or Spiderman's wrist-mounted web-shooter malfunctioned into overdrive."

"You got me, John."

"One to go, where is Captain America?"

"Pfft fraaap poot blat thppthtphphhph braaap braaaack frrrt blaaarp pbbbbt."

"Here, he is behind the huge American fridge-freezer."

"I know it, I shouldn't have eaten baked beans for breakfast. They gave me away."

"Pfft fraaap poot blat thppthtphphhph braaap braaaack frrrt blaaarp pbbbbt."

"Oops, be careful guys, I have just released a toxic gas in the living room."

"Well done Captain America, you have switched off my lightsabre."

"I'm going to open the windows to let some fresh air in!"

"Good idea, John. It stinks in here!"

The old Fiat 500

Mollie loved her old white Fiat 500. She named it Claire. Her car was more than a vehicle to take her where she wanted to be, Claire was her first car. It brought lots of good memories like her first job. Mollie considered her like a reliable friend who never let her down. Claire was compact and easy to drive and park. The interior was functional, and the seats were comfortable. Mollie could not believe nine years had already passed. She was driving in the suburbs of Leeds where the maximum speed was 30 miles per hour. Claire was perfect, apart from being targeted by the police. Mollie heard a siren, and she looked at the rear-view mirror. The police car had flashing lights and siren on full blast.

Nee-naw, nee-naw, nee-naw, nee-naw.

"Driver of the white Fiat 500, pull over!"

Mollie found a free parking space and pulled over.

A police officer stepped out of his car and approached the old Fiat 500. He knocked on the driver's front door window. Mollie rolled down her manual window crank handle.

"Good morning officer, how can I help you?"

"Good morning, madam, do you know why I have pulled you over?"

"How am I supposed to know! If you don't, we are screwed."

"Madam, calm down, less cheek more cooperation! I topped you, because were driving at 95 miles per hour in a 30 miles per hour zone."

"That is absurd, Constable. My car is 9 years old. When I bought it new, its maximum speed was 100 miles per hour. Now its maximum speed is 70 miles per hour after I floor the accelerator. I believe I was driving under the 30-mph speed limit."

"I have no choice but to issue you a ticket for speeding."

"Stop, Constable Matthew Ings, I have checked the digital tachometer laser speed-gun, and it malfunctioned again providing a false reading. Firstly, it measured 95 miles per hour, but after I tapped on the screen, it showed 25 miles per hour."

"Madam, you are free to go. I'm sorry for the inconvenience."

It was the first encounter with the police. Two months later, Mollie was driving on the motorway. The speedometer was on 59 miles per hour. She heard a siren, and she looked in the rear-view mirror. The police car had flashing lights and siren on full blast.

Nee-naw, nee-naw, nee-naw, nee-naw.

"Driver of white Fiat 500, pull over!"

Mollie parked on the hard shoulder.

A police officer stepped out of his car and approached the old Fiat 500. He knocked on the driver's front door window. Mollie rolled down her manual window crank handle.

"Good afternoon officer, I was driving under the speed limit."

"Yes, madam, you were driving dangerously slowly for the motorway. I have no choice but to issue you a speeding ticket."

While the police officer was filling the ticket, a red Ferrari 512 BB sped past at over 120 miles per hour.

"I'm sorry Constable, are you not chasing and asking that car to pull over?"

"No, I'm not. The driver is the most awarded police officer in the region, who is undercover, chasing a criminal in a getaway car."

The South America' s car trip

Giuseppe and Daniele were Italian and had been good friends for over a decade. They enjoyed each other's company, they had so much in common. They were passionate about business, travel, agriculture and they both had a family. Giuseppe had worked for more than 40 years in an Italian bank as a bank manager and during the weekend he spent his spare time in his farm cultivating and irrigating maize or rice.

Daniele was an architect during the week and at the weekend he looked after his winery. They loved exploring new countries. They were getting old. Giuseppe had the idea to explore South America by leasing a car and discovering local food and drinks. Daniele was very keen. Giuseppe took care of everything from booking the flights, hotels, leasing a Jaguar car with comfortable leather seats and spacious legroom. He was in his comfort zone being a control freak and being a boss at work and at home. He felt no one was on his level apart from Daniele. Their friendship was on the same level, so neither was subordinate or superior. Some rumours claimed their friendship was more than platonic, suggesting they were involved physically and emotionally as a gay couple, it was never proved. Giuseppe felt a deep connection with his money. He was overjoyed when he acquired more, he was depressed when his wealth had been squandered. Even though Giuseppe was a multi-millionaire, he was careful with his wealth. His money was his 'precious'. When he spent time with Daniele, his overbearing control of his money had been loosened up. He overcame the challenge of the cost of the South America's car trip by contacting all his friends, who owned hotels or companies in South

America and obtained more favourable deals and coupons. Giuseppe and Daniele were ready for their trip of a lifetime. They had prepared their luggage with all kinds of clothes, shoes and translating dictionaries; they could only speak fluently in Italian. They thought they were so clever they didn't have to learn other languages. They would work out a way to communicate with the locals.

Their journey started on 15 July 2022 catching a direct flight from Milan airport to Caracas, capital of Venezuela, by a private jet owned by Daniele's multi-millionaire friend. After a couples of days rest, they would pick up their leased Jaguar car and start to travel on the west coast. Giuseppe had made a gaffe. He forgot to ask which kind of unleaded petrol the car needed so it performed to its best. There were two options, low or high ethanol. He was confident he would work it out, when he would face the problem. Giuseppe and Daniele enjoyed the local cuisine and South America's scenery.

On the eighth days of the journey, Daniele noticed the fuel gauge.

 "Giuseppe, we have a problem"

"What is it, Daniele?"

"We are running low on unleaded petrol."

"Don't worry, I think I saw a sign further back, there is a petrol station in two miles. While you are going to the loo, I will fuel the car."

Two miles later, they stopped at the petrol station. Daniele went to the loo. Giuseppe had to make a choice between low or high ethanol. The price of the two unleaded was extortionate.

"I am confident the car would work if I fuelled it with low ethanol. I cannot justify paying so much money. Decision has been made."

Daniele returned from the loo.

"Are we okay?"

"Yes, we are. After I am back from the loo, we are ready to carry on with our journey."

The Jaguar transformed from being a jaguar into a tortoise, despite flooring the accelerator, the Jaguar's top speed was now 40 miles per hour. It was creating a long traffic jam of angry motorists behind. They all showed their frustration. Beep beep beep. Each of them overtook the Jaguar expressing their point of view.

"Even my ninety years old grandmother, drives faster than you."

"Who gave your driving licence? A tortoise?"

After nine days, their journey was turning into a nightmare and would now take longer than they expected. The next day, Daniele checked the fuel gauge.

"Giuseppe, I have good and bad news."

"Tell me the bad news, first."

"The bad news is we are running low on unleaded petrol, and the good news is that in the next mile we arrive at another petrol station."

They just had enough unleaded petrol to reach the petrol station.

"Giuseppe, I don't care how much it costs, this time I will choose the unleaded petrol."

"Go for it."

Daniele fuelled the Jaguar this time with high ethanol. The car transformed again from a tortoise to a cheetah. Its top speed was 150 miles per hour making up the time Giuseppe and Daniele had lost previously. The car brought the attention of the police, and they were pulled over more than ten times and received hefty speeding fines.

The holiday was one to be remembered for all the wrong reasons.

Good days and nightmares

The first night…

"Whirr, whirr, whirr, whirr."

"Tat-tat-tat-tat, tatatatatata tat-tat-tat"

The second night…

John was more prepared placing his head under the pillow. The intensity of the noise was overwhelming.

"Whirr, whirr, whirr, whirr."

"Tat-tat-tat-tat, tatatatatata tat-tat-tat"

The third night…

"Whirr, whirr, whirr, whirr."

"Tat-tat-tat-tat, tatatatatata tat-tat-tat"

John wore wax earplugs. They absorbed some of the noise. The following day, John met Andrew in the street.

"Hi John, how are you?"

"Not great, I haven't slept properly for days."

"Are you not getting on with your parents?"

"Yes, during the day we are bonding well, but at nighttime the nightmares begin, my dad snores like an electric chainsaw: *'Whirr, whirr, whirr, whirr'*, and my mother snores like a nail gun: *'tat-tat-tat-tat, tatatatatata tat-tat-tat.'*"

"You are minted; if you opened a furniture shop, you could make tables and chairs, wardrobes, beds and cabinets. I can imagine a couple entering your shop and asking if you could make a bespoke table and chairs. You would reply, of course, we can. Please come back tomorrow afternoon, my parents work night shifts. They make the best furniture while others are sleeping."

Simple maths

Pierino is an 8-year-old Italian boy who lives in Ravanusa in Sicily. He became famous for his ability to solve all kinds of math equations. He wants to live a normal life, and all the attention causes him anxiety. He discovers biting his nails is a way to release all his stress, nevertheless he feels so embarrassed by the state of his hands, and he always keeps them in his trousers pockets.

One day, he is sitting on a school chair in his classroom in a math lesson, when his teacher asked him a math equation.

"Pierino, can you solve this simple math equation? What is it five plus five?"

Pierino counts once. He counts twice. He counts three times in his head.

"Pierino, it is not difficult. You need add all your fingers from your left hand and all your fingers of your right hand."

"Yes, miss, it's 11!"

"No, that is not correct. It's 10"

"Miss, it seems I have gained a new thumb since I have put my hands in my trouser pockets."

Hide and seek take 2

"Today, we have new players: me, an ordinary man, Human Torch, the Invisible woman, Aquaman and Chewbacca. We are playing an old children's game. It is called hide and seek. I am going to close my eyes, and I will count up to one hundred while the players are hiding. Then I open my eyes and find the hiders."

John turned his body toward the wall. His head was leaning on his arm. He started to count loudly.

"One two three four … ninety-seven, ninety-eight, ninety-nine, one hundred, ready or not, here I come!"

John turned his body around with his eyes wide open.

"Rrrraaawwwrrrr, grrrawwwhhh."

"I can hear someone, yes, it's Chewbacca behind the column. Apart from hiding, you shouldn't make any sound, or you give yourself away."

"Rrrraaawwwrrrr, grrrawwwhhh."

"One down, three to seek out. I see you, Human Torch"

"I shouldn't have hidden behind the ice sculpture!"

"You shouldn't have, the children will be disappointed. They took three weeks to create a Zeus ice sculpture and in two minutes you melt it!"

"Please apologise to them."

John noticed something.

"Aquaman, you are behind the fish tank."

"No, I am not, John."

"Yes, you are. All the fishes are staring at you!"

"I told them telepathically to stare at the female fishes in the other fish tank, but they ignored me. Instead, they are staring at me, typical gay fishes!"

"Three people have been found. One to go, where is the invisible woman?"

Her power was starting to fade, and she appeared in the middle of the living room naked. As soon as she realized, the others could see her, she covered her lady parts with her arms and hands.

"Damn, my powers have been on and off this week."

"Rrrraaawwwrrrr, grrrawwwhhh."

"Thank you, Chewbacca for being a gentleman and pass me a towel. I'm so embarrassed."

"You are glad, you didn't say in Spanish *'Estoy embarazada'*, which translates into English as 'I'm pregnant'."

The holy baptism

In Ravanusa, the council had built a public toilet for priests, bishops, archbishops and nuns and another one for atheistic men and women.

Pierino's father had noticed that, for the last three weeks, his son was using the religious public toilet. He observed from a distance and noticed his son behaved carelessly. He took courage and with an inquisitive attitude he sought an explanation.

"Pierino, are you aware we are not allowed to use the religious public toilet?"

"Yes, dad, I know. Three weeks ago, I discovered when I was baptised as an infant, the priest inadvertently immersed my bottom in holy water, making my bum divine."

The number is up

(The Comic sans font is used for talking dogs)

"Who did it?"

"Did what?"

"I'm not going to be mad; if you or Jockey confess what happened to number 2?"

"Jockey and I, we don't know what you are talking about, mum."

"I know you are both talking and clever dogs, but I am not stupid. There are traces of number 2. If either of you confesses within five minutes, there will be no consequences, otherwise both of you will not get treats for a week."

Drops of sweat were falling down Jockey's fur head.

"Okay, I confess. I did it."

"You see, that was not difficult, Jockey Where is it?"

"Mum, is the number 2 a chocolate?"

"Don't be daft, Jesse."

"I ate it."

"That is disgusting, Jesse."

"It smelled a bit, probably it was off. I was so starving; I didn't think twice."

The password

"Peter, have you changed the wi-fi password?"

"Yes, I have, Judith"

"Could you give it to me?"

"I'm not going to tell you."

"Peter, why are you so awkward? You have always been supportive of me. If you don't, we will have no intimacy for a week."

"Last time, we had intimacy, was a year ago."

"Thank you for rubbing it in, I would never do this. I am going to kneel and beg, clean all the dishes for a week and do whatever you say."

"It's sweet, I am not going to tell you."

"You are a horrible person."

Judith pondered; her brain was working overtime.

"Just a minute, I think I got it. It is I am not going…"

"Shhh, don't let others hear it. It's capital I, spaces between words and lower case."

The mechanic

Lewis is a versatile mechanic, he can fix all kind of vehicles: cars, motorbikes, bicycles and buses. One day he was checking the oil in the bonnet of a BMW series 3, when he heard: *jug—jug--spat*, the roaring engine of a Yamaha R6.

Lewis glanced at the motorcyclist, who was wearing a tight black leather jacket, trousers, gloves, a helmet and boots. The rider was tall and slim. The motorcyclist removed the helmet, and it revealed long black straight silky hair. The rider was a beautiful woman with blue eyes and red lips.

"Hello gorgeous, my Yamaha R6 is making a very strange noise. Could you check it for me?"

"Of course, give a minute."

Thirsty minutes later, Lewis had repaired the motorbike. The stunning lass smiled and kissed him on his cheek. Lewis blushed.

Two hours later, Lewis was waxing the BMW series 3.

This time, a Ducati Panigale V4 stopped outside of his service shop. The rider was short, and the leather jacket and trousers were showing off the body's curves. The motorcyclist removed their black helmet revealing long blonde hair.

"I cannot believe, I am the luckiest man in the world. What a chance to meet two beautiful women in one day. Blonde women are my type. Calm down mate."

He felt stiffness in his boxers.

"I am a professional mechanic; I need to control my emotions."

The rider turned their head towards Lewis. The motorcyclist had big bushy eyebrows, a thin curled up moustache and a goatee beard.

"Hello mate, I am having trouble with my motorbike. Can you check it for me?"

"You need to be patient. I have just started my second coat. I'll be with you in half an hour."

In the closet

"Hello."

"Hello, I know everything about you. Your name is James King."

"That is correct!"

"I'm in your house." "Why have you hung up?"

"If you are in my house, we don't need to talk on the phone. We can talk face to face."

"I prefer to hide."

"Are you shy?"

"No, I'm not. I want to scare you. I'm holding a kitchen knife."

"I am trembling with fear."

"Let's play a guessing game. Tell me a room and ask me if I'm there."

"Are you in the kitchen? If you are, you can start chopping the carrots and potatoes. You can prepare a casserole for dinner."

"No, I'm not. I am not cooking for you."

"Pity, are you in the living room? Chelsea is playing against Manchester City this afternoon."

"You are wrong again; I don't care about football."

"Are you in the bathroom? It stinks, I forgot to flush the stools in the toilet."

"Yuck! I'm not in your bathroom."

"So where are you?"

"I'm in your bedroom."

"Where? Under my bed?"

"No silly, I am hiding in your closet!"

"That is impossible, I don't have a closet in my bedroom."

"Bummer, I'm in the wrong house."

Help, help

Jenny took her dog to the park and released its lead. Her dog was running free on the grass.

Twenty minutes later, her dog hadn't come back. Jenny was worried something terrible had happened. She shouted in desperation.

"Help, help!"

Two men, Andrew and Peter, were talking while sitting on a bench and they rushed to her rescue.

"Are you okay, madam?"

"I'm worried about my dog, it disappeared."

"My name is Andrew, and he is Peter. Don't worry, we'll help you to find your dog."

"What kind of breed is it?"

"Thank you, my name is Jenny. It's a Yorkshire terrier. It just loves running in this park. Help, help"

"We'll help you. What is its name?"

"Its name is Help."

"Just a second, I was driving my car ten minutes ago, when I saw a Siamese chased by a Yorkshire terrier. I did my very best to halt my car by pressing the brake. Unfortunately, I couldn't avoid it. I'm so sorry, I ran over your dog. At least, it passed away peacefully. Is there anything I can do?"

Tears were rolling from her eyes.

"Andrew, you could kneel"

"I can do that"

"Then stick out your tongue"

"It's getting weird."

"Now bark"

"Woof, woof"

"Good job, are you good at chasing cats and fetching tennis balls?"

"I have never done it before."

"One thing, dogs can't talk!"

It's a good boy

(The **Bold Italic Comic Sans** font is the dog's thoughts)

Betty was ready to take Jockey for a walk. Her next-door neighbour approached her.

"Hi Betty, is this your dog?"

"Hi Josh, yes, it is. Its name is Jockey. It's a good boy."

"MWahahaha, mum, I appear to be a good boy, but appearances are deceiving. A week ago, while you were in the kitchen, I went to your bedroom and chewed your white fluffy slippers. Then I picked them up with my mouth. I was waiting for the right moment to present itself, when you were talking to your boyfriend on the driveway. I ran out from the sliding doors in the kitchen to the garden where I dug a hole and buried them. That was my first mischief. Two days later, when you were not looking, I marked my territory on your red roses prickly bush. Yesterday, you were talking on your mobile phone, and you were distracted, I sneaked out in the neighbour garden and left a stinky present on their lawn. Now you know, mum, I'm not a good boy, mWahahaha."

Going out for one pint

Logan Drinkwater followed a routine, every Friday at 19:00, he was eating his dinner with Betty, his wife.

"Will you stay out long tonight, Logan?"

"I will go out for a couple of hours, darling. Don't worry."

"I know you always go out for one pint."

"That's right."

At 19:30, he shaved his facial hair and had a shower. He got dressed and walked for ten minutes from his house to a modern pub named The Red Lion.

It was 19:59 in The Red Lion.

"Tonight, Logan is cutting it rather fine."

"I agree with you, Joseph."

Joseph, Andrew and Peter were waiting while sitting on a wooden bench inside the pub.

It was now 20:00.

"Here he is."

Logan had entered The Red Lion.

Peter waved his right hand and Logan approached the group.

"I thought for a minute, he wouldn't turn up."

"I would never miss our gathering. You know that, Peter."

"We know Logan, you are a predictable man. You wouldn't change your routine. For once, why don't you live a little?"

"What should I do?"

"That is the spirit, instead of drinking one pint, let your hair down and enjoy yourself."

"Okay, I am up for it."

"Guys, I have already paid for my first round, down in one!"

All the bottles were clinking.

"Down in one! Guys."

"Good job, Logan."

"What should happen? Peter."

"You should start getting drunk."

"I think this beer is defective. I don't feel anything."

Josh came back with another four pints of beer.

"Try this one, Logan."

"Okay."

Logan drank up the new pint.

"This one is defective as well. Peter, I didn't know you have a twin brother."

"I don't, slow down, Logan, we are catching up."

Logan felt more relaxed. All the worries and responsibilities that were occupying his mind during the day, temporarily vanished. His behaviour and his talk to his friends were indicators that he had broken the chains of inhibition.

"I should have done this before. I feel free to do whatever I want. Hic!"

"Logan is getting drunk."

"I'm perfectly fine. I am not drunk, Peter."

"No at all, Logan. You are sober."

"That's right, hic."

"Logan, you are getting hiccups."

"Damn, hic hic."

"Don't worry, Logan. You can get rid of it. Simply drink another beer."

"Thanks, Peter. I love you guys!"

The DJ was ready to play groovy music.

Logan had an intense desire to express himself on the dance floor. Without hesitation, his feet were drawn to the main stage. Logan was dancing moving his feet and arms to the beat of music.

People were cheering and applauding his performance.

"I was not aware; Logan is a good dancer."

"Nobody knew, this is the first time I have seen him dancing."

"Peter, what is he doing now?"

"Josh, this is so funny. He thinks he is talking to a woman. He is having a conversation with a column."

"Peter, can anyone drag him over here? He is making a fool of himself."

"Wait Joseph, Logan is now hugging the column and attempting to kiss it."

"I'm embarrassed, I'll never come to this pub again."

"Calm down, Peter. The bouncers are escorting Logan outside."

Logan was disoriented and confused. He recognised he was no longer inside the pub. His left foot wanted to be in control of his body, but the right foot had other intentions. Logan allowed his left foot to be in charge for a short period of time. He was zigzagging in the deserted main road. He was wandering without any purpose. Logan decided to consent to the right foot taking charge. Logan appeared to be zigzagging in the direction of his house. He recognised his avenue.

He approached a tree where a wild dog was sleeping.

"Come on, Logan, unzip and aim. I'm sorry dog, I am marking my territory."

Logan zipped up his trousers and moved forward to his house. Before drinking it would take him ten minutes, but now every step seemed daunting and in a slow motion. One hour later, Logan was in front of his squeaking gate.

"Shh, you are waking up all the neighbours."

He was zigzagging on the footpath leading to his front door. He pulled out the key. The keyhole was moving right to left and vice versa. He realised it wasn't, his right hand was shaking making it difficult to insert the house key, so he grabbed his right hand with his left. His uncontrollable shiver subsided, he turned the key and entered his house. The lights were on. Betty was tapping on the wooden floor in the landing with her right slipper. She was wearing her pyjamas. She had a green mask, making her like the Incredible Hulk, and a dozen hair rollers completed the terrifying outfit. Betty had her fists on her waist and her arms akimbo.

"Is Halloween having a comeback? Who left the witch out!"

"I was worried and sick all night, something terrible happened to you. You didn't call, you didn't come back home."

"Should we call the doctor? Are you still sick?"

"Look at the pendulum wall clock. It's 3 o'clock in the morning. Everyone is sleeping, except you. Apologise."

"I'm sorry pendulum wall clock."

"Never mind, I converted the sofa bed. Tonight, you are sleeping in the living room. Good night, Logan."

Logan plunged on the sofa bed, hugging the pillow. During the night, his sleep was interrupted by the dripping water from the kitchen tap and the ticking sound of the pendulum wall clock, every sound of the house was echoing in his head as if someone was playing drums.

Act of kindness

Dear Father Christmas,

My name is Emily Brown. I am ninety years old, and my request is very peculiar. I am not sure if you can help me. I'm desperate. I have tried to ask all my friends for help, but due to inflation and the cost of living, all my friends are struggling financially. I know you are very busy during December building toys for all the children in the world and probably you won't be able to do anything for me. If I don't ask, I will never know. Three days ago, I collected my monthly pension payment of £800 from the post office and I didn't notice a young man was following me. As soon as I was walking in a deserted street, he grabbed my handbag and ran off. It happened so quickly; I didn't have the time to identify the mugger. He was wearing a hooded jacket.

I'm still horrified by the ordeal and the police don't have any suspect or clue on how to solve this crime. I am wondering if you could perform a miracle and help an elderly lady. My pension pays my food, my electricity and gas bills. This year, my friends are coming over for Christmas Day, however I don't have any money due to the mugger. I am really worried about my house being cold during December. I won't be able to pay my heating bill until January. I believe in you.

Emily Brown

P.S.: I'm sorry for the letter being wet and some of my writing being smudged, while I'm writing this letter, tears are dropping on the paper.

Emily posted the letter to Father Christmas' North Pole address. At the post office mail distribution department, James, a postman, came across Emily's letter. He noticed the letter was wet. He thought it had happened during a rainstorm, so he replaced the envelope. He was aware he was not allowed to read the content, by accident he read Emily Brown's letter. He was so moved by the content. He organised a gathering of his work colleagues in the pub after work.

"Thank you for meeting me tonight. I need to ask you a favour."

"It must be very important, James."

"Firstly, I know it is against post office policy to read the content of a private letter. Emily Brown had been mugged, and she doesn't have any money to pay her bills and food. I'm wondering if we can donate some of our salary. I'll pretend to be Father Christmas as she asked for his help."

"James, I will donate"

"Thank you, Josh."

"I will, let's keep this between ourselves."

"Thank you, Andrew."

A few days later, a reply from Father Christmas arrived at Emily Brown's address.

Ho ho

My dearest Emily,

This is Father Christmas. When I read your letter, I was moved to tears. No one should have been through your ordeal. I asked all my friends, and I have filled the envelope with money, hopefully you will not starve this Christmas, and your house will be warm.

Merry Christmas

Father Christmas

Emily was jumping with joy, and tears were rolling for happiness.

A month later, Emily wrote a new letter to Father Christmas.

Dear Father Christmas,

I feel as though I was twenty years old again when I was in love with my first boyfriend. He used to write me love letters every week.

When I saw your envelope, I knew the letter came from the North Pole.

I want to thank you from the bottom of my heart. My Christmas Day was one of the best Christmas I had ever had. The house was warm. I am so glad I had the money, because it had snowed every day in December. I didn't write to you before; you were so busy building toys for the children and bringing the presents on Christmas Eve.

I counted the money three times; I could not believe £100 was missing. I blamed the postman, who is greedy. Probably he saw the money in the envelope and the temptation was too strong. I understand inflation and the cost of living make people act differently, but the postman should not take from vulnerable people.

Emily Brown

James saw Father Christmas' envelope and he recognised Emily Brown's writing. He invited the two other postmen to the pub after work so he could read them the letter Emily had sent to Father Christmas.

At the casino

"I've been doing well tonight; I made £2000 in profits playing blackjack. This hand is very difficult to play. I have in total 15. The dealer has a King of spades showing, I have no idea about their card face down. I can stand or choose to "hit"."

"Mr Johnson, it's your turn. You can stand or receive more cards."

"I know dealer, hit me."

"Pow!"

"Hit me again!"

"Pow!"

"Hit me again."

"Pow"

"What do you have Mr Johnson?"

"I have two black eyes and a broken nose."

"I meant about your cards."

"I forgot about that; I have 19"

"Unlucky, the house wins with 20."

The employer's phone calls

"Warning it's your boss. Your boss is calling you now, don't pick up, if you do, you will be talking to your boss.", it was Andrew's boss calling.

"Hello."

"Andrew, where are you? You supposed to start your shift at 9 a.m."

"Who is this?"

"You know who this is, it's your manager George White."

"Why are you calling me at this time in the morning?"

"Because you are not at your desk."

"Of course not, I am on holiday."

"Who authorised your time off?"

"You did, don't you remember?"

"Okay, I need you in the office now, five people called in sick today and we are short of staff."

"Even if I could, it would be impossible. I am in Australia; it would take me at least a day to fly back to the U.K."

"How disappointing!"

6 months later.

"Warning it's your boss. Your boss is calling you now, don't pick up, if you do, you will be talking to your boss.", it was Andrew's boss calling.

"Hello."

"Andrew, where are you? You supposed to start your shift at 9 a.m."

"That is weird, I am sure I have taken the day off. Let me check my calendar."

"You don't have any holiday booked today."

"Yes, I have. Who is this?"

"You know who it is, it's your manager George White."

"You were my ex-manager; I left your company 6 months ago. We had an exit interview, don't you remember?"

"You are lying, you are still an employee and I'm your boss so stop being lazy and find excuses. Get in the office as soon as possible or you will face a disciplinary!"

"I'm sorry George White, I'm no longer an employee of your company. Please stop contacting me, this is the fifth time you called me this week. You were in a car accident, you have been diagnosed with anterograde amnesia, whereby you only remember everything up until the night before the accident."

What are you in for?

"Welcome to Hell!"

"My name is Seb. I have heard many things about you, Devil. I find you so hot.", licking his lips and winking with his left eye.

"I blame the flames behind me, let me guess, you are in here for being excessively high opinion of yourself."

"Not at all, my opinions always come second to others."

"Okay, I didn't expect that. You have been sent here for an insatiable desire for material gain."

"Devil, again, you are mistaken. Every month I donate part of my salary to charities and help the less fortunate."

"Wow, I didn't see that coming. You are an angry man always hurting or threatening people."

"I'm the most loving and caring person. I will never harm a fly."

"You sound too perfect; I am confident you envy others for lacking skills or achievements."

"I admire others, they are my inspiration for being the better version of myself."

"Even you, you cannot control your animal desires, sooner or later, lust will prevail."

"I'm not like any human. I control my emotions."

"No man or woman can resist over-indulgence and over-consumption of food and drinks."

"My body is a temple. I only drink water and eat healthy food. That is why my body is slim."

"There are days, you will probably be lazy, and you won't care about anything."

"Devil, I care about people every day. My purpose is helping others."

"I'm confused."

The Devil placed his finger in the red rotary phone and called God.

"Stop being a matchmaker, I can find my soulmate on my own. You always meddle in my love affair."

"Devil, I just want to help you. You are so lonely and depressed."

"Is he gay?"

"Yes, he is. He cannot enter Heaven. He almost tempted Saint Peter at the gates."

Grandma

"Emily, where is grandma?"

"Last time, I saw her, she was in the kitchen. She is not here."

"Maybe, she is gone up."

"She is passed away and she is having a cup of tea with grandpa. Rest in peace, grandma."

"Emily, I didn't mean she is dead. Perhaps, she is upstairs."

"She is walking the stairs leading to Heaven."

"Behave Emily, she is not in Heaven."

"If grandma is not in Heaven, is she in Hell with other sinners being poked by the Devil with a trident for eternity?"

"That is awful thing to ask, she is neither in Heaven nor in Hell."

"Mum, is she behind me?"

"Yep, she looks fine to me, but her face is red, and white smoke is coming out of her ears and her nostrils. She thinks she is a dragon."

"Is she having a stroke?"

"I don't think so, she is very mad at you!"

"So, I guess I am not getting a PS5 for my birthday, bummer."

Rome then Mori

"Hi John, how was your holiday in Italy?"

"It was awesome. I visited the Colosseum, the Trevi fountain and the Spanish Steps. I drank lots of wine, and ate pizza, pasta and ice creams."

"I can see you enjoy the Italian food; your tummy is like a dome."

 "The Italian food is so tempting and delicious. I couldn't resist. Are you Italian, Giovanni?"

"Last time, I checked I am."

"Great, someone told me to go to Rome then Mori, I did. I visited Rome then I went North, South, West and East of Rome I couldn't find Mori. I asked the locals where Mori is. Some laughed and others looked at me in a weird way."

"I see, go to Rome then Mori is a colloquial expression which means you go to Rome, and you love living there so much so that you want to spend the rest of your life there until you die. Mori doesn't exist."

Holiday Inn

Aviva acquired a company in Cambridge It had created over hundred vacancies and funded the training, travel costs and hotel accommodation for the new employees who travelled from York to Cambridge for several months.

Within these recruits, Paul Robinson, John White and Mark Brown were staying at the Holiday Inn. Their lives had never crossed before. Their lifestyle was different from each other at the weekend. Paul Robinson was a party animal, and he loved going out to nightclubs and dancing all night. John White was a chess player grandmaster and Mark Brown was a guitarist in a boy band. They had one thing in common they loved exploring and tasting new food. They met in the restaurant in the Holiday Inn and became good friends. They tasted all the dishes on the menu.

A week ago, the restaurant was celebrating Mexican food.

The waitress approached the table.

"Hello gentlemen, are you ready to order?"

"What can you recommend, Miss?"

"Well, our best dish is fajitas with peppers. I need to warn you, the green peppers are very spicy."

"I love living dangerously, I laugh at spicy food. I order one fajitas por favor."

"We know, John. Let's make it two."

"If John and Mark order fajitas, I'm in. We are like three musketeers."

"Okay, gentlemen, there fajitas coming up. In the meantime, should I take your drink orders?"

"We are okay at the moment."

Half an hour later, the waitress returned with three fajitas dishes served with green peppers.

The three friends were digging in.

"I don't understand the fuss of the green peppers. They are not very spicy."

"John, the green peppers are very tasty, you need to be careful of the seeds, which contain strong spices giving you a burning sensation in your mouth."

"Hot! Hot! Call the fire brigade - there is a fire in my mouth."

"Mark has just chewed one of the green peppers seed."

The waitress was running and approached their table.

"May I get you some drinks?"

"Yes, please can I get a jug of water?"

"Any more drinks?"

"The jug of water is just for me. You need to ask my friends about their drinks."

Freeze frame

"I'm bored, John."

"Auntie Suzie, let me finish the dishes. I'll make a cup of tea, and we'll have a game of Scrabble. Meantime why don't you watch TV. There is a documentary on BBC2 talking about the sea flora and fauna in ten minutes."

"This old crap TV set, it's not working again!"

"That is odd, I repaired it last week. You are lucky, I'm a TV technician. Have you tried to turn the TV off and on again and select a channel?"

"John, I've been for the last ten minutes. Every channel has the same documentary about the sea flora and fauna."

"I'm nearly finished the dishes. Be patient, Auntie Suzie, I'll sort it."

John entered the living room.

"Auntie Suzie, that is not your TV, it's the fish tank."

"Are you sure? It has lovely pictures. I cannot see properly without my glasses."

"They are sitting on your hair."

Auntie Suzie picked them up and placed them on her aquiline nose squeezing her eyes.

"Now, it's all making sense."

At the restaurant

Jack and Jenny are having a dinner date at Weatherspoon's restaurant in York.

"Jenny, I have some great news. I'm sorry I have been a pain all week. I have been stressed out at work. We had a presentation for a new client, who is minted. If we acquire this contract, the company will make lots of money. My team and I secured the contract. I promised you a great holiday, last year, and if money was not an object, I would take you to New York, your favourite city in the world, for a week, do you remember?"

"Yes darling, I love New York, it is a city which never sleeps. Can we go?"

"Of course, Jenny, I received a large bonus, and I booked a week off as annual leave. We are going to New York, are you excited?"

"Oh yes, oh yes!"

Three tables away from the happy couple, another couple were having dinner. Carl took his wife Katy to the same restaurant he wanted to treat her to some healthy food without the drama and the stress of cooking.

Katy overheard Jenny's excitement and called the waiter.

"Yes madam, are you ready to order?"

"I would like the same meal as that woman."

"May I have a double?"

"Double, are you crazy Carl?"

"It has been a tough day for me, I need all the treats I can get."

"No problem, sir and madam."

Fifteen minutes, the waiter returned and placed a plate in front of Katy and two plates in front of Carl."

"I beg your pardon, waiter, where is the food? The plates are empty."

"That couple has not ordered yet."

The loan

"Tring tring"

"Hello, I'm Jennifer from Santander, how may I help you?"

"I'm Paul Robinson. I am calling about the outstanding loan I took out several years ago."

"Before I can discuss the loan, you need to pass the security questions."

"Go ahead."

"Thank you, can you confirm your full name?"

"My name is Paul Robinson."

"Great, what is your date of birth?"

"My date of birth is 03 July 1963"

Great, finally, can you confirm your full address including your postcode."

"3 Fanny Avenue Sheffield S21 1AY"

"Great, I can now access your loan account. How can I assist you?"

"I have never missed a payment for the loan as you can see from your system."

"That is correct."

"Unfortunately, my circumstances have changed. My employer has reduced my salary by £3000 a year. I reduced my outgoings and cancelled direct debits. Even with these changes, I cannot continue to pay £150 a month towards the loan."

"I'm sorry to hear about your current financial situation. Santander is proud to listen to the customers and offer solutions in every circumstances. How much can you pay every month to reduce the capital and interests?"

"I have been through all my income and expenses and after paying Council Tax, rent, utility bills and groceries, I am left with £10."

"I understand, your current balance is £10,000, if you keep paying £10 a month, after eighty-three years your loan will have been repaid. Hopefully, your circumstances will improve in the future, and you'll be able to pay more and clear off the loan sooner."

"Hopefully, I have been applying for new jobs, which pay more than my current employer."

"Is there anything also I can do, Mr Paul Robinson?"

"No, at all, bye bye Jennifer. Thank you for your help."

"It's my pleasure. We are always here to help our customers."

Six months later, Paul Robinson called Santander. After he passed the security questions, he explained the reason of his call.

"Great, Mr Paul Robinson, I can now access your loan account. How can I assist you?"

"Thank you, Andrew, I have called you today, because my circumstances have changed. I started a new job last month and it pays me more than my previous employer. I want to increase my repayment for the loan. Currently, I'm paying £10 a month."

"That is correct."

"I want to pay £100 a month, how long would it take me to clear off the loan?"

"Let me calculate it for you, the computer says 70 years."

"Mr Paul Robinson, are you still there?"

"Yes, I'm sorry, I fell off the chair. Are you sure 70 years? How can it be?"

"When we changed the terms and conditions, some fees and penalties had been applied to the loan. They caused the debt to increase. You can still pay more every month, and it will reduce how long it will take to clear off the loan."

"I understand, but if I keep paying £100 a month, I will be dead before the loan will be repaid."

The invisible man

In the science community, there was only one man who had the highest IQ and the ability to achieve scientific advancement for humanity. His name was Ethan Cunningham. For the last ten years, he was working tediously on an invisibility formula. He was so obsessed with his invention, he only craved for perfection, nothing less. If he didn't achieve it, the science community would tease him for the rest of his life. On 4 September 1997, in his laboratory basement, an excited scream had been heard.

"Eureka! Finally, after many years of attempts and failures, I have achieved the formula for invisibility. Any object will become invisible for a short period of time. Before I spray this formula on living tissue, I will test it on an inanimate object like this apple."

Ethan sprayed the invisible formula on the red apple. The apple gradually faded and vanished from the visible light spectrum. Ethan grabbed his phone, selected the clock app and tapped the start of the stopwatch. Ten minutes later, the apple became visible on the table. He checked if the apple had been altered by the formula. It was like nothing had happened to it.

"Now, it is time to test it on live tissue."

Ethan grabbed the bottle with the invisible formula and walked out of his terrace house. He was strolling on the pavement when he came across the post office. He entered the building and noticed a young woman wearing a tight dress showing off her curves, waiting to be called next to the counter. Behind her and, supported by a walking stick, an eighty-year-old man's lip was blowing hair, and his right arm was shaking by the long wait.

"This is the perfect time for testing my new invention!"

Ethan sprayed the formula all over his body - like a woman before she was going out. His body gradually faded and vanished from the visible light spectrum. He approached the young woman, slapped her bottom and pulled up her dress, showing her knickers.

The elderly man smiled broadly.

The young woman's face turned red, and white smoke was coming out of her ears.

"You, behave!"

"I haven't done anything."

"Sure, you slapped my bottom and pulled up my dress!"

The young woman regained composure turning her body around still waiting to be called to the counter.

"I have not finished yet, let's prank this young woman and elderly man even more."

Ethan spanked the young woman's bottom even harder and undid the elderly man's belt and trousers, his trousers fell on the floor revealing his boxers, which exclaimed *'I'm a party animal'*. The final act of Ethan was to push the elderly man towards the young woman, who turned her body in anger. The elderly man's hands, by mistake, grabbed her breasts.

"You filthy animal, take your hands off my breasts. You are a pervert! You should be ashamed of yourself."

The investment

Paul Robinson was only eight years old when his dad, Joseph, a bank manager and qualified investor, suggested that he opened a saving account in the bank in which he was working. Paul trusted him, because his dad showed knowledge and confidence in making the right choices for investments, but he wished he had never done it.

"Paul, let me open a saving account for you and every year you will receive interest."

"Okay, dad, I trust you."

Every year, Paul continued to give all his pocket and birthday money to his dad, who recorded it in a bank book. His saving account grew.

At the age of eighteen, Paul was in a college where he was studying Accountancy, and his favourite subject was Banking. He learned how to invest, and he wanted to put into practice the knowledge he acquired.

One day, when he came home, he approached his dad.

"Dad, today at school, we learned how to invest our money. Yesterday, I became an adult, and I would like to make my own investment decisions."

"You are an ungrateful son, for ten years I have been looking after your money and adding interest to your saving account. I have many years of experience in investing and now you think you are better than me. How dare you!"

Joseph's face turned red and white smoke was coming from his ears. Joseph calculated a value in his mind.

"I have been generous; I am giving you an extra £150 as interest on top of your current balance of £1,500. You should be grateful."

When Joseph mentioned the interest, Paul believed £150 per ten years was a good return of investment. He was naïve and gullible. With more maturity and knowledge, Paul realized he had been scammed from his dad. During the ten years, his dad was controlling his money, other investments offered a better return around 10% a year comparing with his miserable 1%.

Paul had to endure a waiting time. One month later, his dad had forgotten to pay him. Two months later, Paul was still waiting. Three months later, Jospeh woke up and handled £1,650 to his son.

"What are you going to do with these money? I hope you are not spending it on clothes or music?"

"No, dad, I'll invest it."

Paul went to another bank and the bank clerk suggested that he invested an equal proportion of his money every week into an equity fund. This would allow the investment to compound and reduce the cost of the equity purchases.

Every day Paul checked the equity fund on the internet, and his investment was increasing in value. After four months, he went to the bank, he had decided to withdraw the entire investment making the same amount of profit which had taken his dad ten years. He had no choice, if he had left the money invested in the equity fund, he would receive less than he invested.

His dad was aware of his son investment's success, because his wife was disclosing all the financial activities Paul was undertaking.

"Well done son, I have heard of your investment success. Are you ready to join the big boys? I have done a good job looking after your money for ten years."

"Let me think, for ten years you had my money, and my return of investment was a miserable 1% per year, I achieved the same value within four months. Are you taking me for a fool? I rather prefer to be run over by a bus than give you all my savings again."

"I come back to you."

Spanish misunderstanding

Roberto Dicuore worked for an IT company, which had a branch in London in UK, but the head office was based in Madrid in Spain. The company was implementing new procedures to all the branches and requested some of the staff to travel to Spain. The IT manager chose Roberto, who was the brightest member of his staff, to travel to the head office. The head office paid Roberto's flight, accommodation and food expenses. For a week, Roberto stayed at the Spanish chain hotel, Ibis. Before he travelled, he almost became a fluent Spanish speaker. He assumed Italian and Spanish are similar languages so if he couldn't remember the Spanish word, he could say an Italian word instead. He would be okay.

Roberto arrived in Madrid late afternoon, and he checked in at the hotel. The following day, after having a shave and shower, Roberto got dressed and took the lift. He was in the breakfast area. He previously ordered a Continental breakfast. On the table, four toasted slices of bread, a jug of milk for his bowl of cornflakes, a glass of orange juice, a teapot and a strawberry jam were waiting for him.

He was searching on the table for some butter, there was no sign.

"Hola camarero (Hello waiter)"

"Sí, señor (Yes, sir)"

"¿Puedo tener algunos (Can I have some) burro (butter)"

Roberto could not remember the Spanish word for butter, so he used an Italian word, not knowing the two words have different meaning.

"¿Burro, ¿está seguro señor? (***,are you sure sir?)"

"Vamos! (let's do it)"

"Sí, señor (Yes, sir)"

Five minutes later, the waiter returned with a donkey.

Hee haw, hee haw

"Camarero, ¿Puedo tener algunos más burro (waiter, can I have more butter)"

"Sí, señor (Yes, sir)"

Five minutes later, the waiter returned with another donkey.

Hee haw, hee haw.

"Why is this waiter bringing me more donkeys? Where is the butter?"

"Sir, I can speak English, in Spanish burro means donkey!"

"Now, I understand, I couldn't remember the exact word, so I used the Italian word instead."

It's raining cats and dogs

"I don't think you should go out. It is pouring down."

"Don't worry, Jack. Water never harms anyone. Without water, there would be no life."

Fork lightning lit up the sky followed by a thunder rumbled above their house. Drops of rainwater were pounding on the window.

"I'm Mr Waterproof! My hood is waterproof as are my jacket and trousers. Water is going to bounce over my clothes."

"If; you are sure."

"I am, Jack."

Trevor sighed, opened the front door and stepped out.

Five minutes later, Trevor walked back in with ripped clothes. His heart was hammering in his chest, and the rest of his body was shaking like a leaf.

"Don't go outside!"

"Are you okay, Trevor? What happened to you?"

"I'm okay. It's raining."

"I know it is. I can hear it."

"You don't understand, it's raining cats and dogs, literally. As soon as I stepped out of the house, a St Bernard dog fell from the sky and jumped on me. Siamese cats scratched my jacket and trousers. The worst was still to come. An Egyptian evil cat appeared from nowhere. It seemed so weird without fur but docile. I stroked his head, you know I love cats, but not anymore. I shouldn't have done it. My action made it mad. Its appearance was deceiving. The Egyptian cat was a kung fu master. It grabbed me and threw me on the floor several times with precise martial arts. It kicked me on my chin with his back paw and flipped 360 degrees. His back paw kicked my little "Freddie." It added that 'no one dares to touch me, I'm the kung fu master'. It extended his claws and scratched every part of my body."

"Poor, you, Jessica will be very crossed with you. You have not been intimate with her for three months."

"Tell me about it, I'm very sore down there."

They sat on the sofa and saw a cat stretched out, sliding on the glass with his tongue out. In their street, all the neighbours heard evil domestic animal sounds.

Meow! Meow! Meow! Woof! Woof! Woof!

Winter is coming

On the North American reservation, the Sioux tribe was preparing for the winter.

"Sitting Bull, what kind of winter do you think we will have this year?"

"Chief Red Cloud, three years ago, it was mild. Two years ago, the temperature was around 0° C, last year, it was bitterly cold."

"I can see a cold trend."

"The spirits foresee a mild winter."

The Indian tribe was not convinced, it chopped more wood, fearing the worst.

Two days later, Chief Red Cloud approached Sitting Bull.

"Have the spirits foreseen a warmer winter?"

"I'm afraid, the spirits predicted the winter will be not as cold as last year."

The chief Red Cloud motivated the tribe to chop even more wood.

Three days later, the chief Red Cloud approached Sitting Bull.

"We are prepared for the winter."

"I talked to the spirits again, which predicted the winter will be freezing. They based their prediction on how much wood the tribe had chopped."

Six months later, it was a bitterly cold winter. Many male Indian Sioux were infatuated by the youngest woman, Kimimela, nicknamed Butterfly, who had the deepest black eyes and perfect smile, which melted all the male hearts.

"Sitting Bull, I can see you are not immune to Kimimela's charm and beauty. You are aroused."

"Not at all, Chief Red Cloud, it is the freezing cold stiffening my body."

The snooker frame

The night before…

"Jack, I'm going out."

"Great, have a great time, Jessica."

"Are you not asking with whom?"

"Who are you going out with?"

"It's me and the girls. so no guys allowed, and we'll probably party all night. I'm starving though, I am thinking I will eat something in the pub."

"Awesome."

"Are you not asking me what time I am coming back?"

"What time are you coming back?"

"I am not sure yet, maybe around 10 p.m. or early morning next day. The girls and I always lose track of time."

"It's cool, early or later, I'll be sleeping."

The following night…

"Jessica, I'm going out."

"Where are you going, Jack?"

"I'm meeting up my friends at the snooker club."

"What time are you coming back?"

"I don't know."

"Will you eat in the snooker club?"

"Yes, I'm starving. Why are you asking all these questions?"

"I'm curious, can I come along?"

"Of course, you can, but I thought you said snooker is boring to watch."

"I cannot stand watching other snooker players. I love watching you playing snooker. I love being around you all the time. That's what girlfriends do."

"Okay, if you are ready, let's go."

"I'm so excited."

Jack and Jessica walked into the snooker club. Jack was carrying a replica of Ronnie O'Sullivan's snooker cue.

Inside the snooker club, Mark and Frank were waiting.

"Guys, you don't mind Jessica watching the snooker frames."

"Not at all."

"Can I ask a question?"

"Go ahead, Jessica."

"The purpose of the frame is to pot a red, followed by a colour, until you have more points than the opponent. You then win the frame."

"That is correct, Jessica."

"I'm not just a pretty face. Anyone can do this."

"Just a moment, it looks easy on TV, snooker players have been through an Academy and every day they practice for eight hours."

"I wish I could have a go."

"Jessica, my only concern is you could rip off the cloth on the table. If you do, I will need to pay for it."

"Don't worry, Jack. I will be careful."

"Let your girlfriend have a go."

"Thanks Mark."

"I want to see this."

"Have faith in me, guys."

"It is your turn, Jessica. Next ball is a red. There are three red balls next to the bottom right pocket, two red balls next to the cushion and two red balls next to the bottom left pocket. I'm confident you will pot a red ball or at least not miss a red ball."

"Thank you for the confidence, Mark."

Jessica positioned her left hand on the table and stroked the cueball with the aim of hitting a red ball, but she miscued it. The cueball rolled towards the three red balls near the bottom right pocket, but it avoided all of them. Next it moved toward the two red balls near the cushion, again it avoided contact with any red ball. It now moved closer to the two reds near the bottom left pocket. The cueball missed any contact again.

"That is incredible, I never saw such a poor shot in my life. The chances that a snooker player could miss eight easy reds are astronomical!!"

"I'm sorry guys, when I watch snooker on TV, snooker players are potting balls with ease."

***** you and me

In Birmingham, every year, an international convention invites entrepreneurs from all over the world to share business ideas, knowledge and collaboration.

The most established entrepreneur was Mr John Brown, and he was attending. During the fifteen minutes break, John approached twin: a Japanese brother and sister

"Hello." He smiled and waved.

They both smiled and waved.

"Are you brother and sister?"

They nodded.

"Great, they cannot understand me. I'm John Brown.", touching his chest with his hand.

"I'm John Brown", they repeated.

"I'm John Brown, what is your name?"

"I'm 'I fock you'."

"Thank you for sharing, I am straight. You should be careful in expressing your sex orientation in this venue. Some people might find it offensive. What is your sister's name?"

"I'm 'you fock me'." She replied.

"This must be a family disposition. You should be washing your mouth out with soap. Be careful, someone might spank you. In a more discreet place and convenient time, I would be intrigued."

"No John, you misunderstood, when our parents were young, they visited North America and heard everyone was saying our names. When they returned to Japan, these phrases stuck in their mind and thought it was a good idea to use them to name their son and daughter. In Japan, our names don't mean anything."

A Dalek is upon on us

During his life, Paul Robinson had more than sixty jobs, including cleaner, shop assistant, Accountant and Purchase Ledger clerk. Recently, he became a paperman delivering the local newspaper on foot. He enjoyed the fresh air and the exercise, helping him to lose weight and keep him fit. The job offered another benefit; releasing stress, usually, the curse of every job. It was an easy job; his task was to put the newspaper in the customers' letter boxes. He worked Mondays to Saturdays, and he rested every Sunday. He found he was safe walking on pavements, his friends suggested he rode a bike, so it would take him less time to complete the job, but Paul was not convinced. Riding a bike on the road was too dangerous. Cars, buses and motorbikes seemed not to notice cyclists and several cyclists had been killed by cars. Even on a pavement, sometimes Paul was not safe. Some mobility drivers believe they own the pavement, exceeding the speed limit of four miles per hour and other times some young cyclists, didn't suppose to ride on pavements, they overtook Paul without giving any warnings.

Paul was always aware of his surroundings, and he saw many people on the pavements apart from cyclists, mothers with prams and people walking with their dogs. Paul was always strolling in every kind of weather: sunny, windy and rainy days. He was afraid of the winter, the temperature plunged below 0° C, and the pavement was covered by frost and ice making it very slippery. On 4 January 2024, it was the coldest day of winter. It was -4° C, Paul was prepared. He was wearing thermal socks, two jumpers, a scarf, a winter hat and thermal gloves. He was delivering the newspapers when he was dumbfounded.

He saw a young Chinese man, who was wearing sandals without socks, shorts and a t-shirt.

"Blimey, he thinks it is summer. Brr! If I was not wearing my clothes, I would be freezing."

Every week, Paul encountered the recycling truck. One week, he was delivering his newspapers, when he heard the truck speaker saying, "Stand clear this vehicle is turning left", but the sound of the message was a distinctive metallic, robotic staccato sound like the archenemy of Dr Who.

"I didn't know a Dalek was driving the recycling truck."

"Exterminate the black wheelie bin, Exterminate!"

The blind man

"Jack, I'm going to the women's changing room. You can join me."

"I don't know if I should. The other ladies would be very uncomfortable seeing a man while they are taking their clothes off."

"I understand, but I will never forgive myself if someone steals from you while I'm away. I will explain to them that you are blind and gay."

"That is not completely true."

Jessica accompanied Jack to the gym's female changing room, but before he entered the room, she left him near the door.

"Ladies, my best friend Jack is blind and gay. Is it okay if I let him in?"

"Jessica, are you sure Jack is blind?"

"Yes, Linda, the doctor confirmed he is blind as a bat."

Jack entered the changing room supported by Jessica. He was looking straight ahead, making sure his eyes were not wandering around.

A fat naked woman was walking by, making her cellulite dance and her bottom shake like a jelly.

"OMG! She is a big woman; she would be too heavy sitting on my lap. Oh, no my little "Freddie" is turned off."

In one hour, Jack saw many shapes of bottoms: fat, peachy, slim, and breasts: flat, round, long, no man had such a chance in his entire life.

Drops of sweat were rolling down his forehead and his face turned red like a strawberry.

"Are you okay, Jack?"

"I'm fine. When you have so many people in the same room, it creates heat."

"I'm almost dressed, Jack. We will go soon."

One hour later, Jessica drove Jack to his friends' house.

While she went to the kitchen to get a drink from the fridge, Jack was talking to his friends.

"How was your day, Jack? It must be so horrible being out and you cannot see anything."

"Mark, in a manner of speaking, today I had a revelation, my eyes were opened to a new world. I cannot tell you anything, because I swore a secret pact."

Other Publications: Entertainment

Tickle Heart Vol.1

This is a collection of English funny short stories.

Thrumming Heart.

This a spellbinding English collection of fantasy, sci-fi, detective, and paranormal short stories. It received a bronze medal in the Global Book Awards in 2021 and it became an Amazon best-seller in December 2022. The book is available in e-book, paperback, and audio book formats. It will be available as a graphic novel in the future.

Timothy Divine and His Adventures:

These are the first books:

Timothy Divine and Hilo

Timothy Divine and Filo

Timothy Divine and the Comet Kay

These are my first English novels, and they tell the story of Timothy Divine, a 10-year-old boy exploring new worlds in his rocket ship and interacting with his grandfather, Jo, and his friends. The novels have a lot of funny and emotional moments, which I am sure the reader will enjoy and share with family and friends.

Dr Victor Slater and The World.

This is my second English novel, in which the author tells how Dr Victor Slater and humanoid dinosaurs worked together to protect Earth from the invasion of an evil alien race, Y42. In this novel, the reader will come across a love triangle, comedy, and drama.

www.ingramcontent.com/pod-product-compliance
Lightning Source LLC
Chambersburg PA
CBHW071009120726
47910CB00004B/1451